Little Hands Creative STICKER Play

Fairy Princesses

All inquiries should be addressed to:
Barron's Educational Series, Inc.
250 Wireless Boulevard
Hauppauge, New York 11788
www.barronseduc.com

First edition for the United States and Canada published in 2014 by Barron's Educational Series, Inc.

First published in 2014 by Carlton Publishing Group, 20 Mortimer Street, London, W1T 3JW United Kingdom

Copyright ©2014 Carlton Books Limited

ISBN: 978-1-4380-0396-2
Library of Congress Control No.: 2013950645

Product conforms to all applicable CPSC and CPSIA 2008 standards. No lead or phthalate hazard.

Author: Fiona Phillipson
Designer: Kate Wakeham
Illustrator: Jennie Poh

Manufactured by Leo Paper, Heshan, China

Date of Manufacture: December 2013
9 8 7 6 5 4 3 2 1

PICTURE CREDITS
Stock.XCHNG pages 9, 10, 16-17, 25

BARRON'S

Come fly with us!

Meet Sophie, Phoebe, Pippa, and Clara.
They are best friends! Give each one a tiara and then
decorate the fairy forest with flowers, hearts, and bows.

My name is Sophie!

I'm Phoebe!

HOW TO USE THIS BOOK

You'll find over 1000 stickers in the middle of this book, so get creative and start sticking! Some pages need specific stickers to complete the pictures and puzzles. This logo with the page number will show you where to find them on the sticker sheets.

2-3

Call me Pippa!

I'm Clara!

3

Flower garden

Phoebe and Sophie are fluttering through the palace gardens.
Fill the flower bed with beautiful flowers.

Through the looking glass

Clara is getting ready for a party at the palace. Can you make her reflections match by adding five finishing touches to the image on the right?

Find the stickers in the middle of the book

5

ANSWERS ON PAGE 64

5

Flying fun

Four princesses want to go flying with their fairy friends!
Stick the royal girls into the floaty hot air balloons,
then fill the sky with butterflies, birds, and dragonflies.

Find the stickers
in the middle
of the book

6–7

Precious pets

Find the stickers in the middle of the book

8

The fairy princesses are playing with their adorable pets! Stick the correct creature on top of each shape.

ANSWERS ON PAGE 64

8

Flag fun

Some important visitors are expected at the palace today!
Stick flags on the turrets to make them feel welcome.

Sparkly shopping trip

This is Phoebe's favorite shop in the Fairy Kingdom! Look at the signs then fill the shelves with the correct items.

Find the stickers in the middle of the book

10

Sleeping beauty

Sssh! Sophie is asleep! Find pretty stickers
to complete the patches on her cozy quilt.

Find the stickers
in the middle
of the book

11

Follow the clues

Find the stickers in the middle of the book

12

What image belongs at the end of each string of hearts?
Use the three clues to help you guess.

ANSWERS ON PAGE 64

Come to the party!

You have been invited to Princess Clara's birthday party.
Decorate the invitation as beautifully as you can.

You are invited to a

Sparkly Princess Party

at the palace.

Hope you can make it!

Love Clara x

Fairy wishes

Sophie is going to make your wishes come true!
Find stickers of some of the things you might wish for.

Shadows on stage

What magical dancers! Stick the correct fairy princess on top of each shadow, then decorate the rest of the stage.

Find the stickers in the middle of the book

15

ANSWERS ON PAGE 64

A fairy feast

Inside the palace kitchens, the royal chef is preparing for a grand banquet! Use your stickers to add lots of food and kitchen items to the scene.

What to wear?

Phoebe and Clara are helping these princesses get ready for a grand ball. Choose stickers to make each one look party perfect!

Find the stickers in the middle of the book

18

Pretty hands

Find bright, sparkly rings and dainty bracelets for these royal hands. Use your stickers to give the nails a manicure, too!

Home sweet home

Phoebe's bedroom is very messy! She's looking for four missing things, can you help her find them? Once you spot each item, put a sticker next to it on the missing items list.

Find the stickers in the middle of the book

20

ANSWERS ON PAGE 64

Missing items

◯ teddy bear

◯ bouncy ball

◯ flowery slippers

◯ golden crown

Skating friends

Sophie and Pippa love skating around the frozen lake, but they get cold quickly. Find some nice cozy clothes and hot drinks to warm them up.

Where's my wand?

Sophie and Pippa are about to fly off to a party. Find a wand for each of them, then add lots of magical stars.

Off to the ball

This princess is on her way to the ball, but she's lost her way. Stick carriages along the path that will take her to the palace.

Find the stickers in the middle of the book

23

ANSWER ON PAGE 64

Underwater magic

Tabitha is a water fairy. Find the correct stickers to match the eight shapes so she can play with her ocean friends.

Find the stickers in the middle of the book

24

ANSWERS ON PAGE 64

Fun in the sun

The summer beach party begins at sunset and the fairy princesses can't wait! Stick on some ice creams for them to enjoy while they relax.

Dancing after dark

The sun has set and the music is playing. This is the one night that Tabitha becomes a land fairy! Fill the scene with beach party stickers.

Time for tea

These fairies are enjoying tea and cakes! Use your stickers to complete the missing parts of the picture.

Find the stickers in the middle of the book

28

ANSWERS ON PAGE 64

Birthday baking

Sophie, Clara, and Pippa have made a flying birthday cake for Phoebe. Add some decorations to make it even more magical.

Pick a pair

Find the stickers in the middle of the book

30

Princesses love shoes! Can you find the missing stickers to complete each pair? Now stick four matching handbags on the shelf underneath.

ANSWERS ON PAGE 64

Gems and jewels

Fairy Princess Phoebe was given this fabulous tiara for her birthday.
Decorate it with sparkly gems and shiny jewels.

Dolly dress-up

Pippa's favorite dollies are called Milly and Molly.
Can you find some pretty clothes to stick on
Milly so that she matches Molly?

Find the stickers in the middle of the book

32

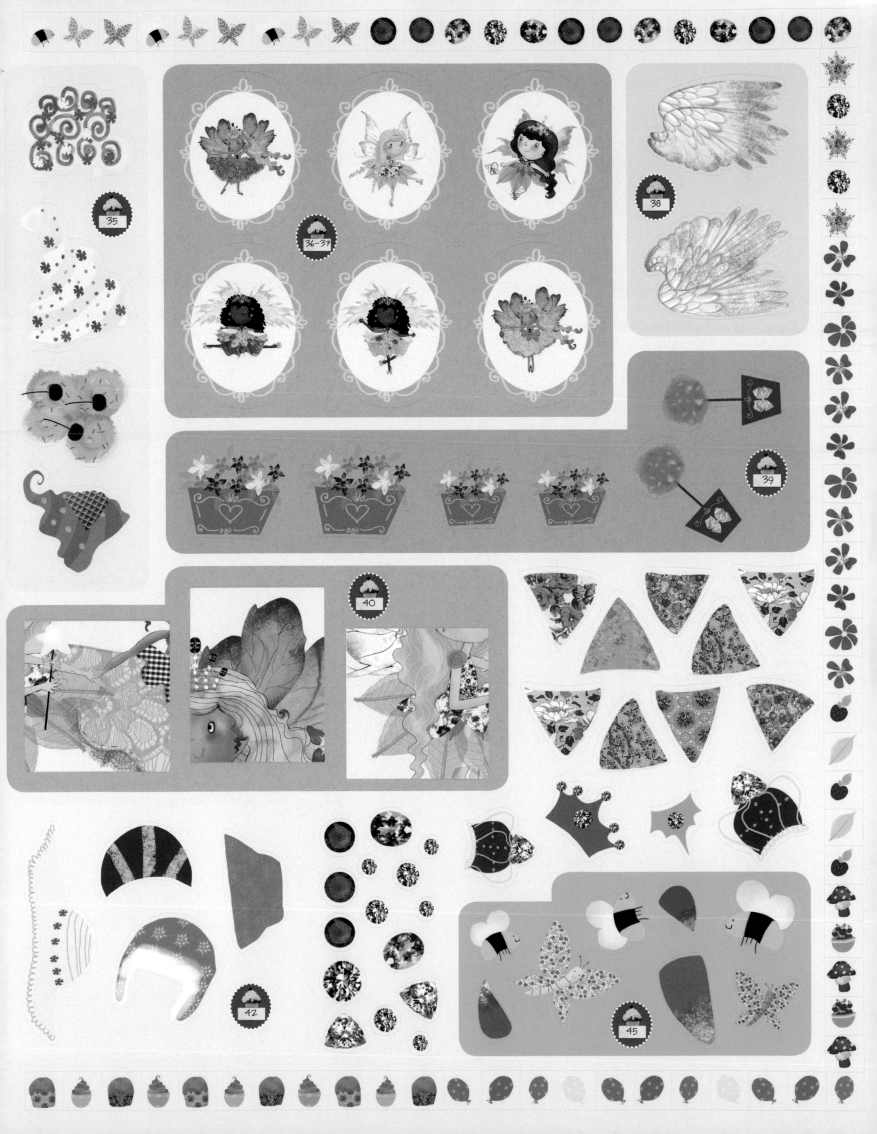

Potions for a princess

Take a look inside Princess Sophie's beautiful bathroom!
Now fill the shelves with fairy brushes, perfumes, and potions.

Royal ice-cream parlor

Clara visits the royal parlor every Saturday.
Stick some toppings on her ice-cream sundae,
then add more goodies to the shop window.

34

Cupcake fantasy

Sophie and Clara have been baking!
Decorate their yummy cupcakes with
colorful icing swirls.

Find the stickers
in the middle
of the book

35

Come dance with me!

Tra-la-la! The four friends are perfecting their dance steps for the ball. Look at the pictures and then find the missing sticker for every routine.

1

2

3

ANSWERS ON PAGE 64

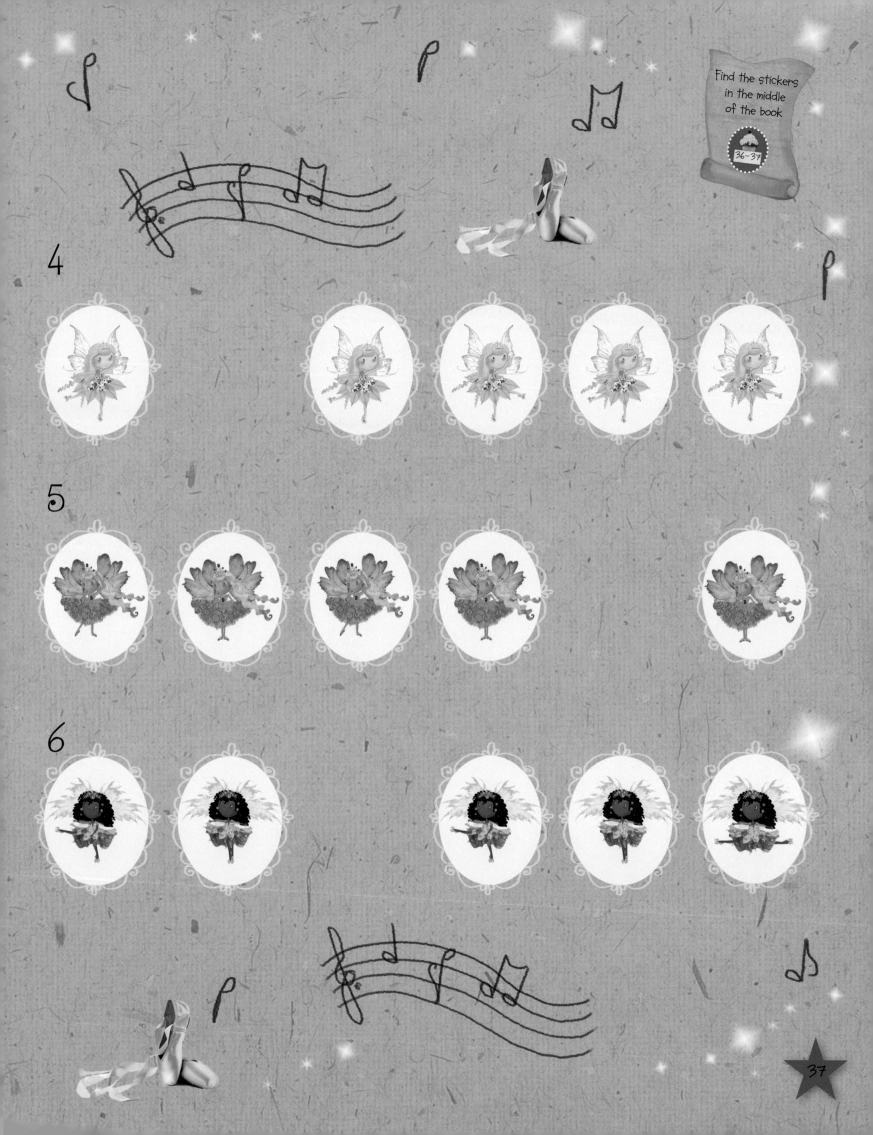

Find the stickers in the middle of the book 36-37

Enchanted animals

Find the stickers in the middle of the book

38

Clara and Pippa are feeding the animals at the petting zoo. Stick on wings to transform these creatures into magical unicorns!

Castle makeover

Help Fairy Godmother give this castle a magical makeover. Add pretty window boxes, then put two trees outside the door.

Find the stickers in the middle of the book

39

Friends in a frame

Clara and Phoebe are best friends. Find the stickers that match the picture on the right, then carefully place them into the fairy frame below.

Find the stickers in the middle of the book

40

ANSWERS ON PAGE 64

Party perfect

Help the fairy princesses get ready for their party.
Stick a row of patterned bunting between
the trees.

41

Find the stickers in the middle of the book

42

Heads and hats

The fairy princesses need new hats! Read the clues,
then put the right sticker on each friend's head.

Clara loves her scooter!

Wrapped up for winter

Pippa's enjoying the sun

Dancing in the rain

ANSWERS ON PAGE 64

Salon style

Phoebe's family has an appointment at the royal hairdresser's! Top off each person's smart new look with a shiny sticker crown.

Wonderful wings

Sophie wants her wings to look super sparkly today!
Use stickers to decorate them with twinkly precious gems.

Flower fairies

These tiny fairies live in a plant pot in the palace garden!
Stick on the missing flower petals then decorate the
page with bees and butterflies.

Find the stickers
in the middle
of the book
45

Find the stickers in the middle of the book
46

Magical masterpieces

Phoebe is at the art gallery, choosing a painting for her mom's birthday. Put a sticker picture into each of these fabulous frames.

Roller royals

Sophie and Pippa are looking for something amazing
to wear to the royal roller skating party.
Help them find the perfect outfits.

Cloud spa

Fairy princesses adore being pampered!
Decorate this cloud spa with bubbles, brushes,
and other beauty bits.

Beautiful bedtime

Sophie is wishing for a pretty new bedspread. Can you design one for her? What stickers will you choose?

Super sunset

These fairies have gathered to watch the sun set.
Find a pair of gorgeous wings for the smallest one.

Find the stickers
in the middle
of the book

51

Hide and seek

Find the stickers in the middle of the book

52

Pippa is looking for her three adorable pet kittens.
Can you find them on the sticker sheet?
Stick each kitten onto a bed.

Midnight feast

Clara and Sophie are having a slumber party—they can't wait to share their magical, midnight feast! Fill the page with yummy fairy treats.

Find the stickers in the middle of the book

Funny bunny!

Look at these pictures of Sophie and her fluffy bunny. Add five stickers to make the bottom picture perfectly match the top one.

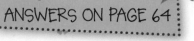

ANSWERS ON PAGE 64

54

Cupcakes and bubbles

There's a posh party at the palace tonight! Stick in a royal butler, then add trays of cupcakes and fizzy drinks.

The fairy festival

Can you find ten magic star wands hidden in this busy picture?
Place a pretty heart sticker over each one.

ANSWERS ON PAGE 64

Find the stickers in the middle of the book

56-57

57

Find the stickers in the middle of the book

58

A wonderful wedding day

Welcome to this fabulous fairy wedding.
Clara, Sophie, Phoebe, and Pippa are bridesmaids!
Give each friend a posy of flowers to carry.

Magic by moonlight

Decorate this beautiful nighttime scene with four stars, three fireflies, two sleeping birds, and one glowing moon.

Find the stickers in the middle of the book

Follow the flowers

Clara is stuck in the garden maze! Can you show her the way to the picnic table? Leave a trail of flower stickers along the right path.

ANSWER ON PAGE 64

Find the stickers
in the middle
of the book

60–61

Find the stickers in the middle of the book

62-63

Fairy races

Which of our fairy friends has won this thrilling flying race? You decide! Give your favorite a winner's rosette and a beautiful bunch of flowers.

Answers